# Belinda the Ballerina

by AMY YOUNG

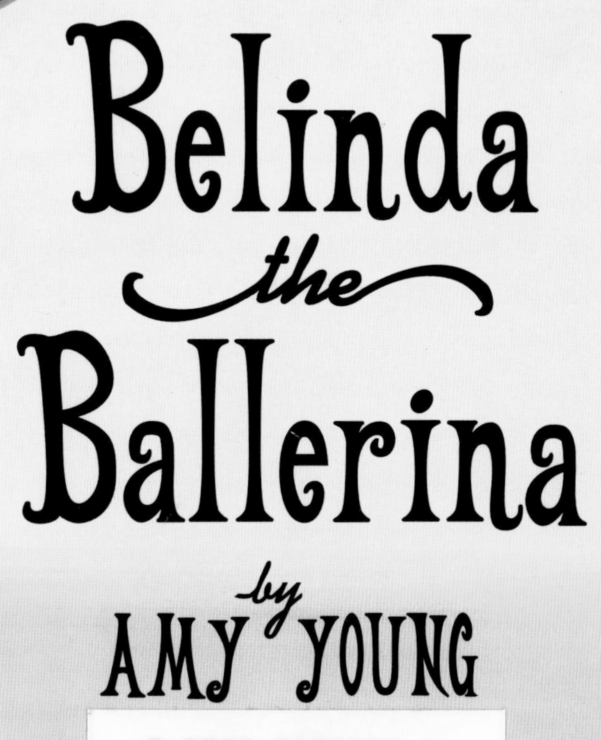

To my mother and father

VIKING
Published by the Penguin Group
Penguin Putnam Books for Young Readers, 345 Hudson Street, New York, New York 10014, U.S.A.
Penguin Books Ltd, 80 Strand, London WC2R ORL, England
Penguin Books Australia Ltd, Ringwood, Victoria, Australia
Penguin Books Canada Ltd, 10 Alcorn Avenue, Toronto, Ontario, Canada M4V 3B2
Penguin Books (N.Z.) Ltd, 182-190 Wairau Road, Auckland 10, New Zealand

Penguin Books Ltd, Registered Offices: Harmondsworth, Middlesex, England

First published in 2002 by Viking, a division of Penguin Putnam Books for Young Readers.

1 3 5 7 9 10 8 6 4 2



LIBRARY OF CONGRESS CATALOGING-IN-PUBLICATION DATA
Young, Amy.
Belinda, the ballerina / Amy Young.
p. cm.
Summary: When Belinda auditions for the Ballet Recital and the judges tell her she cannot be a ballerina because her feet are too big, she tries to forget about dancing.
ISBN 0-670-03549-1
[1. Dance—Fiction. 2. Foot—Fiction. 3. Ballet dancing—Fiction.] I.Title.
PZ7.Y845 Be 2002 [E]—dc21 2001008395

Printed in Hong Kong
Set in Mrs Eaves Roman, Weehah
Book design by Teresa Kietlinski

The illustrations for this book were created using gouache
on Fabriano Uno soft press watercolor paper.

Once there was a ballerina named Belinda.

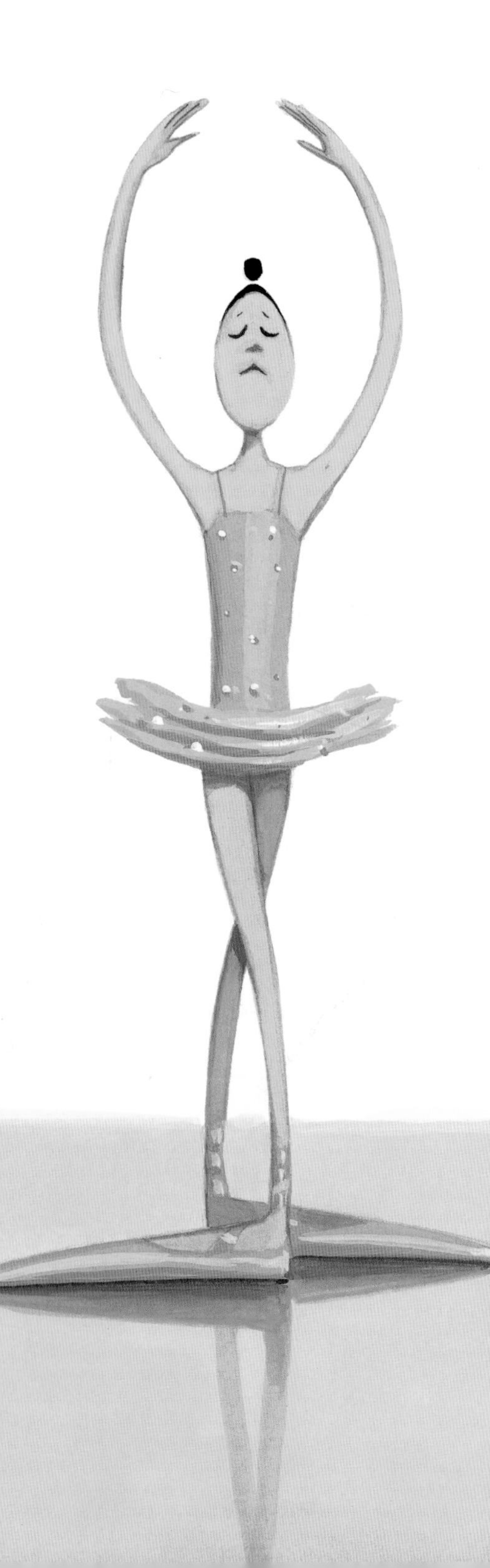

Belinda loved to dance. She went to dancing school every day and practiced very hard. She was graceful and light on her feet.

But Belinda had a big problem—
**two** big problems:

her left foot and her right foot.

Her feet weren't a problem as far as Belinda was concerned. But they were a problem at the audition for the Annual Ballet Recital.

The judges took one look at her feet and yelled,

**"STOP RIGHT THERE!"**

"Egad!" said Sir Fostercheese the Third. "Your feet are as big as boats!"

"They're like flippers!" said George Peach Crumbcake, the noted New York critic.

And Winona Busywitch, who wrote for all the dance magazines, just shook her head and stared.

Belinda didn't even get to audition. The judges said, "Go home. You will never be a dancer—not with those feet."

Belinda was sad. She stayed sad for a long time.

"Maybe the judges are right. Maybe my feet *are* just too big for a dancer," she thought.

So Belinda stopped dancing.

"I'm giving up ballet," she said to herself.

Since she was no longer dancing, she needed something else to do. But she didn't know how to do anything except dance. After looking and looking, she found a job at Fred's Fine Food.

The customers liked
her because she was
quick and light on
her feet.

Fred liked her too,
because she worked hard.

Belinda liked Fred and the customers,
but she missed dancing.

One day a band came to play at Fred's Fine Food. They called themselves Fred's Friends. Before the restaurant opened, they warmed up with a snappy toe-tapper.

Belinda tapped her toes.

Then they played a sweet yearning lilt of a tune,
and before she knew what she was doing . . .

Belinda was dancing!

The musicians came back to play every day, and every day Belinda danced to their music before the customers arrived.

Then one day Fred asked Belinda if she would dance for the customers. Belinda smiled and said, "Oh my, yes!"

The customers were enthralled. They loved it so much that they told their friends, who came to Fred's Fine Food the next day.

And *they* loved it so much . . .

that they told *their* friends, and soon Fred's Fine Food was packed every day with people who wanted to see Belinda dance.

Word finally reached the Maestro from the Grand Metropolitan Ballet. He came by for a look because a friend of a friend told him that he really must see Belinda dance.

He was impressed.

He was touched.

He was moved.

"You must perform at Grand Metropolitan Hall!" he cried. "Please say you will!"

Belinda laughed and said, "Oh my, yes."

The customers cheered.

So Belinda went to Grand Metropolitan Hall and danced to the sweet music of Fred's Friends. She loved to dance!

"Magnificent!" the judges cried. "We have discovered a swallow, a dove, a gazelle!"

They didn't even notice the size of her feet.
They were too busy watching her dance.

Belinda was happy, because she could dance

and dance

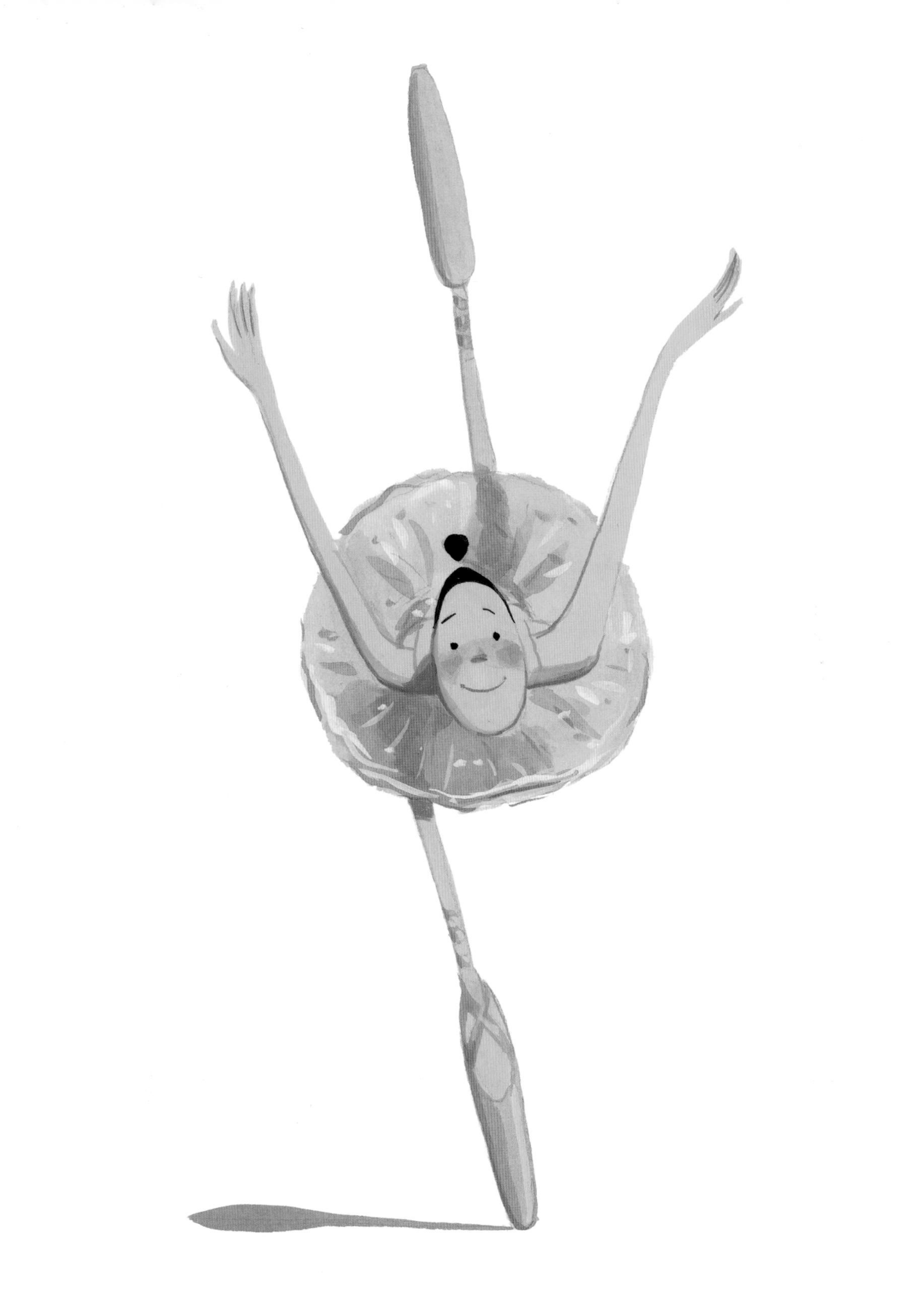

and dance.

As for the judges, she didn't care a fig!